Oswald J. (Oswald Joseph) Reichel

# English liturgical vestments in the thirteenth century

Being a paper read before the Exeter Diocesan Architectural and Archaeological

Society at the College Hall, Exeter, September 13, 1895

Oswald J. (Oswald Joseph) Reichel

**English liturgical vestments in the thirteenth century**
*Being a paper read before the Exeter Diocesan Architectural and Archaeological
Society at the College Hall, Exeter, September 13, 1895*

ISBN/EAN: 9783741183249

Manufactured in Europe, USA, Canada, Australia, Japa

Cover: Foto ©Andreas Hilbeck / pixelio.de

Manufactured and distributed by brebook publishing software
(www.brebook.com)

Oswald J. (Oswald Joseph) Reichel

**English liturgical vestments in the thirteenth century**

# ENGLISH LITURGICAL VESTMENTS

Seal of Thomas à Becket, archbishop of Canterbury, A.D. 1162–1170. The *alb* and *stole*-ends are seen below; above them is the *dalmatic*, the sleeves of which are seen at the elbows; the *maniple* is attached to the wrist; the upper garment is the abbreviated *planet* or mediæval *chasuble*, and an unusual ornamented *pallium*. *See* note 39.

# ENGLISH
# LITURGICAL VESTMENTS
## IN THE THIRTEENTH CENTURY

Being a Paper read before the Exeter Diocesan
Architectural and Archæological Society at the
College Hall, Exeter, September 13, 1895

BY

OSWALD J. REICHEL, M.A., B.C.L., F.S.A.,

AUTHOR OF
"MANUALS OF CANON LAW,"
"SOLEMN MASS AT ROME IN THE NINTH CENTURY,"
"THE SEE OF ROME IN THE MIDDLE AGES,"
ETC.

JOHN HODGES
BEDFORD STREET, STRAND, LONDON
1895

*The writer desires to express his thanks to the Rev. Father Thurston, S.J., for the use of the six blocks which serve as illustrations.*

À *LA RONDE, near LYMPSTONE, DEVON*
13th September, 1895

# CONTENTS

In tracing the origin of these vestments three questions must be dealt with :

### I. THE ORDINARY DRESS OF THE CLERGY.

1. The Roman citizen's dress consisted of (1) an under-garment and (2) an upper garment or planet. The under-garment with sleeves was called a tunic, or without sleeves a rochet (colobus). Those who held any position in society wore between the two (3) a dalmatic . . .

IV. Origin of the Liturgical Vestments.

# ENGLISH
# LITURGICAL VESTMENTS

IN the year 1250, Walter Gray, archbishop of York,
published a series of Constitutions " to the honour
of God and the present information of the Church
of York, and to the memory of all that are to
come," in the first of which he ordained " that
all our parishioners be so well informed in the
following particulars as that they do in all respects
observe them—*i.e.*, the chalice, the mass-book, the
principal vestment of the Church, the chasuble, alb,
amice, stole, maniple, girdle, with three towels and
corporals, and other decent vestments for the deacon
and sub-deacon, according to the condition of the
parishioners and the Church, with a silk cope for the
principal festivals and two others for presiding in
choir at the festivals aforesaid . . . . the frontal for
the high altar, three surplices, a decent pix, &c."

In a Constitution of uncertain date, some thirty
years later, archbishop Peckham of Canterbury,

having evidently in his eye the Constitution in force in the Northern province, published a like Constitution "for the memory of those that are and the instruction of those who shall be," in which, after stating that there is a "dispute between the rectors of churches in the province of Canterbury and their parishioners concerning the various ornaments and things of the Church," he directs all to "know and observe in the following manner, viz., that the missal, chalice, principal vestment of the Church, chasuble, clean alb, amice, maniple, girdle with two towels, cross for processions, lesser cross for the dead, bier, censer, lanthorn with a bell, Lenten veil, manuals, banners, bells, stoup, vessel for salt and bread, osculatory, Easter-taper and candlestick, bells in the steeples with ropes, fonts with lock and key, repairs of the body of the Church within and without, as well in altars as images, glass windows, together with the fence of the churchyard, belong to the parishioners. All other particulars and ornaments, with the repairs of the chancel within and without, ought to be found by the rectors or vicars according to the divers approved ordinations and Constitutions."

"By this it appears," says the Rev. John Johnson,

" that the parishioners of the province of York were bound to find several things which in the province of Canterbury were left to be provided by the incumbents, especially all the books and the vestments, excepting one set for the mass."

Again, in the year 1305, a series of provincial Constitutions was published by archbishop Winchelsea at Merton in Surrey, in the fourth of which it was contained : " That the parishioners of every Church in the province of Canterbury may for the future certainly know what repairs belong to them, and they may have no disputes with their rectors, we enjoin that for the future they be bound to find all the things underwritten—*i.e.*, a lesson-book, a song-book, a gradual-book, psalter, crozier, ordinal, missal and manual, a chalice, the principal vestment with the chasuble, a dalmatic, a tunic, a choral cope and all its *appendages*, a frontal for the great altar with three towels, three surplices, a rochet, a cross for processions, &c."

Lyndwood (p. 252), commenting on this Constitution in the year 1429, declares that by the term *appendages*, used in connection with the choral cope, are to be understood the alb, amice, girdle, stole, and maniple ; and since these vestments are mentioned

in the earlier Constitution of archbishop Gray, and
from the evidence of the service books[1] appear to
have been regularly in use from a very much earlier
date, there can be little doubt that he is right.[2]

From these Constitutions it is clear that in
the 13th century, and for some time previously,
not only were certain garments customarily used
for liturgical purposes in both provinces in this
country, but that they were deemed so necessary
that they were ordered to be provided by the
parishioners. The garments named in both provinces
for the use of the parochial incumbent or ministering
presbyter are : (1) the principal vestment or cope, the
chasuble or planet (Lyndwood, 252), and the
maniple ; the stole is only mentioned in the Constitution of the Northern province, though it is
prescribed in another Constitution of the Southern
province for ministering the Eucharist to the sick ;
and (2) the alb, amice, and girdle. The three or
four first-named garments constitute the distinctive
liturgical dress of the higher clergy ; the alb, amice,
and girdle were worn by all the assistant clergy as

[1] Leofric Missal, p. 59, A.D. 1024.
[2] In Sparrow's "Inventory of the Plate and Vestments of St. Paul's,
in A.D. 1245," appear the words, "*vestimenta et eorum pertinentia.*"

well. In addition, the Constitutions of both provinces mention (3) surplices, not necessarily intended to be worn simultaneously with the garments named,[3] but alternatively at less solemn functions ; and (4) the Constitution of the Northern province requires besides three other copes for festival use, whereas the Constitution of the Southern province requires only one other cope and a tunic and dalmatic. May we infer from this variation that, after the substitution of public and quasi-solemn masses for the ancient solemn Eucharists, some difference of opinion prevailed as to the liturgical costume proper for the deacon and sub-deacon ? In the Northern province copes appear to have been provided for both, as well as for the priest ; in the Southern province, on the other hand, the deacon and sub-deacon appear to have worn the dalmatic and tunic respectively.

In endeavouring to trace the origin of these

[3] Durandus, however, Bishop of Mende A.D. 1286 (lib. iii. c. 2), mentions it as the practice of some to wear a surplice under the amice, and this statement is confirmed by the Forma degradandi clericum in Maskell's Monumenta Ritualia (ed. 1882), vol. ii. p. 333: As the assistants take off the chasuble, the bishop says, " We deprive thee of the sacerdotal rank." As they take off the stole, " We deprive thee of the diaconal rank." As they take off the maniple, " We deprive thee of sub-diaconal rank." As they take off the alb and amice, "We deprive thee of the rank of collet." As they take off the *surplice*, " We deprive thee of the rank of singer."

B

vestments, which it is needless to say were those commonly used in all churches of the Roman obedience since the decree of Pope Leo IV. in 847 A.D.,⁴ it will be well to set ourselves to answer three separate questions, viz. :—(1) What was the ordinary dress of the clergy in ancient times? (2) What if any was the original liturgical dress? And (3) what badges of distinction, authority, or service were from time to time introduced as marks of the clerical order? In so doing we shall do well to remember by way of precaution that the same word does not always denote the same garment when used in different parts of the Church⁵ or even in the same part of the Church at different epochs.

---

⁴ Labbé, viii. 33 : " Let no one sing mass without amice, without alb, stole, maniple, and chasuble."

⁵ Thus *amictus*, or amice, was used by the Roman clergy to describe the napkin or sudarium which was first put on over the bare neck, as Amalarius says, lib. ii. c. 17 (in Le Brun, p. 42), to protect the chest and voice ; by the Gallican clergy to describe the tippet which did duty for the head-band. *Superhumerale* was used by the Roman clergy of the tenth century to express the clerical tippet which the Gallicans called amictus; by the Roman clergy of the sixth century to describe the pallium or band which passed round the shoulders and hung down before and behind. *Casula* was used by the Roman clergy to describe the clerical frock, by the Gallican clergy to describe the ἀμφίβολον or chasuble, the particular form of the planet which was worn by bishops and presbyters in the liturgy. *Tunica* was used in some places to describe the alb; at Rome to express the coloured under-garment of deacons and sub-deacons. *Tunica talaris* in some places to express the

## I.—THE ORDINARY DRESS OF THE CLERGY IN ANCIENT TIMES.

1. At Rome in the fifth century the ordinary dress of all persons holding any position above the labouring class consisted of (1) an under-garment of linen called *linea*, and (2) an upper garment or circular gown enveloping the person, called *paenula*, and in later times *planeta*. The under-garment was sometimes made with sleeves, when it was called *tunica ;* sometimes without sleeves, when it was called *colobus, colobion,*[6] or rochet.[7] Those who held any position of dignity or office wore also on state occasions between the colobus and paenula a third garment of richer material and with wide sleeves called a *dalmatic*. Lyndwood (252) says it was so called because it was first made in Dalmatia. A law of the Theodosian code (xiv. x. 1), A.D. 397,

---

clerical alb; at Rome to describe the cassock. *Stola* was used by Roman writers to express the walking planet or gown; by Gallican writers to express the stole.

[6] Cassian (l. c. 5) requires monks to wear *colobia* in order that they may be free to work. Egbert's Excerpt. 153 : A Roman canon, Let whatever presbyter comes into Church without his colobion and cope . . . . be excommunicated." Isidor (lib. xix. c. 32): "It is called colobion because it is long and sleeveless." The king is vested in one at his coronation. Maskell, Mon. Rit. ii. 25.

[7] Lynd. 252.

forbids senators to appear at Rome wearing a
chlamys or military cloak, and directs them to wear a
*colobus* as an under-garment, and a *paenula* as an
outer garment. Possibly the third Council of
Orleans, A.D. 538, may have had this law in view
when in its 29th Canon it forbad men to attend the
Eucharist dressed in martial costume. Magistrates
when exercising their functions wore over these
garments the *toga*. Their officials, who otherwise
wore the same dress, were distinguished from their
principals, (1) by wearing a girdle round the waist
to confine the tunic ; and (2) by wearing a scarf of
some conspicuous colour as a badge of office. This
scarf, which was called a *pallium*, was sometimes
worn over the *tunic*, and at other times over the
*paenula ;* and it has been suggested by M. Duchêsne,[a]
from whom the above particulars are taken, that the
scarf or pallium may be the abbreviated remains of
the toga.

2. With the exception of the toga, the dress of
Roman clergy in the fifth century was identical with
that of laymen of corresponding rank. The bishop
and deacons wore ordinarily the colobus or rochet as
an under-garment, and the paenula or planet as an

---

[a] Origines du culte Chrétien, 366.

upper garment. On state occasions they wore a
dalmatic between the two. The lower clergy wore a
tunic and planet, but their tunic was a close-fitting one

FIG. 1.

Mosaic from Classe (Ravenna) showing archbishop vested in
rochet and *planet*; above them the *pallium*. The sleeve of
the *dalmatic* is seen over the colobus and under the planet.

and reached to the feet, and was confined with a
girdle, like the garment which we now call a cassock.
The planet was ordinarily of some dark colour,
brown **or** purple; the tunic of a lighter shade, but

not white. This costume was still worn by laymen of distinction in the sixth century. The biographer of Fulgentius relates that on that bishop's return to Africa from exile in Sardinia in 523 A.D., rain happened to fall, whereupon the nobles who had come down to meet him held their planets above his head to shelter him.

That these three garments were also the ordinary dress of a bishop in the third century, may be seen from the proconsular Acts,[9] which give an account of St. Cyprian's martyrdom in 258 A.D. They describe how (1) he took off his shepherd's cloak (lacerna byrrho Conf. Concil. Gangra, 355 A.D. ap. Gratian, 1 Dist. xxx. c. 15)—*i.e.*, his outer garment, *paenula* or *planet*—and knelt down and prostrated himself in prayer before the Lord. Then, when he had (2) divested himself of his dalmatic and given it to the deacons, he stood there (3) in his linen garment. That the ordinary dress of the Roman clergy was not distinct from that of laymen in the fifth century may also be gathered from the letter addressed by pope Cœlestine (A.D. 422–432) to the Gallican bishops,[10] in which he blames them for wearing mantles and

[9] c. 5 in Duchêsne, p. 368.
[10] Ep. 4, ap. Constantium, p. 1067 ; Jaffé, p. 369.

girdles, "as being contrary to ecclesiastical use. We must be distinct," he says, "from the people in doctrine, not in dress; in conversation, not in costume; in purity of mind, not in decoration of the body." M. Duchêsne (p. 366) has also pointed out that the absence of a distinctive costume at Rome for the clergy may be inferred from the long explanation which is given of the meaning of Aaron's sacerdotal vestments in the ordination-prayer, which dates from the fifth century. John the deacon, moreover, in his Life of St. Gregory the Great portrays both Gregory and his father Gordian as dressed exactly alike. Both have on dalmatics; both wear over them planets of a dark colour,[11] yet the one was bishop of Rome, the other a layman.

Fig. 2.

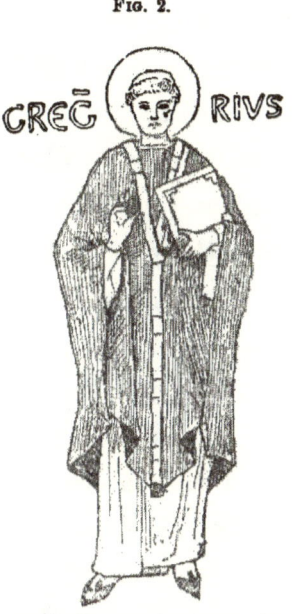

Miniature of tenth century (Stutgardt), showing St. Gregory the Great vested in *dalmatic* and *planet* (the tunic is underneath concealed from view), and wearing the *pallium* passed round the neck and looped.

[11] Duchêsne, p. 367.

3. It is nevertheless abundantly clear that when
after the seventh century the tunic, dalmatic and
planet ceased to be worn by laymen, they continued
to be worn by the Roman clergy, and were introduced into this country and elsewhere in consequence
as the distinctive clerical dress. There exists a letter
from Pope John VI. to the archbishop and clergy of
England (in Haddan and Stubbs, iii. 264), written
about the year 704, in which that Pope states that
all the leading men (*proceres*) of the English who
were then visiting St. Peter at Rome, having met
together, and the arguments *pro* and *con* having
been thoroughly threshed out, they had decided to
fall in with the views of the Holy See so that all the
English clergy on the vigil of St. Gregory had of
their own free will laid aside not only the layman's
flowing habit, but also the whole long dress, and had
taken to wearing tunics reaching to the feet [*i.e.*,
cassocks], according to the Roman custom. He
therefore calls upon the English archbishop and
bishops, as being integral members of "our holy
Church," to lay aside lay vestments and to assume
clerical insignia (infulæ) according to the custom of
the Roman Church." [12]   Out of England the Council

[12] A Constitution of Langton, No. 30, A.D. 1222, decreed by the

of Mainz (Can. 28) in 813 A.D. decreed : " Let presbyters never lay aside the stole (*orarium*) because of the distinction of the priestly dignity." The Council of Tribur, A.D. 895, is said to have ruled [13] "Let not presbyters go abroad unless vested in gown (*stola*) and stole (*orarium*). The decree of Leo. IV., A.D. 847,[14] which ordained, " Let no one presume to sing masses in a planet which he wears in common," shows that the planet was then used alike as the ordinary and as the liturgical garment by presbyters.[15]

authority of the fourth Lateran Council that "archdeacons, deans, all parsons and dignitaries, all rural deans and presbyters, go in a decent habit, with close-copes." Const. 14 of Otho, A.D. 1237, also decreed that clergymen "be compelled by the bishops to that form of apparel for themselves . . . . that was enjoined in the General Council, so that they have garments of a decent length, and that those in Holy Orders use close-copes, especially in the Church and before their prelates and in assemblies of clergymen, and such as have rectories with cure of souls everywhere in their parishes." Lyndwood (p. 119), writing A.D. 1429, observes that these Constitutions were never put in force in this country, and that " common observance prevails over a Constitution, and excuses from it." He also observes (p. 117) that " although certain colours (such as red and green) and certain shapes are forbidden, yet in this country clergy have no fixed habit assigned to them, either in shape or colour, and therefore they may wear any kind of dress which is suitable to their estate, provided it is not expressly forbidden."

[13] Ap. Gratian Cam. xvii. Qu. iv. c. 25.

[14] Labbé, viii. 33.

[15] This is implied in the Constitution of Otho quoted above, in note 12. The Rev. John Johnson, commenting on Const. 30 Langton, says: " It is evident that the close-cope . . . . was a garment of the same make

We may therefore conclude that, so far as the Roman Church is concerned, (1) the tunic, dalmatic and planet were originally the layman's dress, worn alike by clergy and laymen, by Christians and heathen ; (2) that, having fallen into disuse among laymen in the seventh century, they continued to be worn by the clergy, and were introduced elsewhere as the distinctive clerical dress ; and (3) that after the ninth century and before the thirteenth they had become the liturgical costume of the clergy.

## II.—The Original Liturgical Dress of the Clergy.

Can we, then, say that originally the clergy had no special liturgical dress ? On the contrary, there seems reason to say that the use of a liturgical dress was formerly more extended than it is now, being shared by all of the laity who took part in the Eucharistic offering as members of the royal and priestly body the Church. This will, I think, be seen by considering the early baptismal ceremonies.

with the officiating cope. . . . . I infer this from the words of the Lateran Council, viz., ' Let clergymen wear garments close in the upper parts. . . . . Let them not wear copes with sleeves in divine offices in the Church, nor anywhere else, if they are beneficed presbyters.' "

1. Any one who is familiar with the baptismal rite as it was celebrated in both East and West during the first four centuries is aware that solemn baptism was always understood to consist of three parts: (1) the baptismal preparation, sometimes called the sacrament of exorcism[16] but usually spoken of as catechism;[17] (2) the saving laver,[18] or purificatory washing, called the sacrament of the water; and (3) the imposition of hands,[19] called also the sacrament of the chrism.[20] Each of these parts had an elaborate ceremonial of its own, differing more or less from place to place. But among all the diverging ceremonies three stand forth as being in universal use; (1) the vesting the newly baptised in a white garment; (2) the putting in his hand, as one of the illuminated,[21] a lighted taper; and (3) the placing on

---

[16] Augustin (Serm. 227) calls it the sacrament of exorcism. Justin (1 Apol. c. 61, A.D. 140) speaks of the baptismal preparation.

[17] Baeda (ii. 14) relates that Edwin in 627 A.D. built a (wooden) church with his own hands whilst he was receiving catechism and instruction. Constitution 3 Peckham, A.D. 1281, calls it catechism.

[18] Cyprian de Vest. Virg. c. 23; Reichel's Manuals of Canon Law, p. 24.

[19] Heb. vi. 4; Concil. Elib., A.D. 305, Can. 38; Leofric Missal, 222.

[20] Augustin contra Petilian, iii. 104.

[21] Heb. vi. 4; x. 32, Concil. Laodicea, A.D. 363, Can. 47. The Apostolic Constitutions extend the use of the term to those who have been fully exorcised and are about to be baptised; Reichel's Manuals of Canon Law, 36.

his head a royal headband. Thus attired he advanced for the first time to take part in the Eucharistic service and to share in the exercise of the priesthood of the whole Christian body.[22] And thus the white garment, the lighted taper, and the royal headband appear to have been the earliest liturgical insignia of all Christians. Such, indeed, was the importance attached to the use of the lighted taper that the Council of Elvira in 305 A.D. forbad catechumens who had not as yet received the washing of regeneration to light one at all (Can. 37). For this reason a light was always placed before the bishop at every liturgical synaxis. For the same reason, a lighted taper was carried before the deacon when he advanced to the pulpit to read the Gospel, and each one of the faithful who contributed to the common offering held a lighted taper in his hand.[23]

The general use of the white garment by laymen,

---

[22] Hieronym. adv. Luciferianos, c. 4: "Baptism is the priesthood of the laity." Isidore de Eccl. Offic., ii. 25: "The whole Church is consecrated with the annointing of the chrism." Rabanus, A.D. 834, de Cler. Inst., c. 29: "After baptism a white garment is given to the Christian, designating innocence and purity. . . . . After the sacred unction his head is covered with a mystic veil."

[23] In the Gallican Church the layman who offers the materials for the Eucharist may still be seen kneeling at the altar with a lighted taper in his hand.

and particularly by the newly baptised at Easter and for seven days after, is well known; but it seems that in the first ages of the Church the white garment was not confined to Eastertide, but was regularly used by all Christians at every solemn liturgical gathering, at least by all who offered. For in the fourth century we read of long processions taking place in the churches of the Resurrection and of the Apostles at Constantinople, at which the clergy were vested in white garments, "white and more brilliant than those worn by the people."[24] This statement very distinctly implies that the people wore white garments as well as the clergy. However this may have been, at the regular offering days, Easter and Pentecost, laymen were in this country required to wear them by a rule of archbishop Theodore,[25] in 673 A.D. Hence Baeda (ii. 19), A.D. 730, relates that Edwin the King of Northumbria's children were baptised in 627 A.D., and were "snatched out of this life whilst they were still in their white garments," *i.e.*, before Easter week was over. And he also states

[24] Batifol, Histoire du Brevaire, pp. 28 and 39.
[25] Poenit II. xiv. 11, in Haddan and Stubbs, iii. 203, " Out of regard for regeneration, let prayers be said at Pentecost in white garments, as well as in the post-Easter season (Quinquagesima).

(v. 7) that King Caedwalla died at Rome in 689
A.D., "being still in his white garments." As late
as the ninth century Amalarius says :[26] "At Easter
we wear white garments from Sabbath to Sabbath,
and are called alb-wearers (*albati*)." And Eckehardt
(Franc. Orient. Hist. ii.), describing the conversion
of Duke Rollo in 919 A.D., says that after his baptism "he wore his white garments for seven days ;
on the eighth he put them off."

The other article of dress worn by all the baptised
as a liturgical vestment was the royal headband. It
consisted of a broad piece of linen, which was put
over the head to safeguard the place anointed with
the chrism[27] and tied round the neck. It appears to
be referred to by St. Paul in his Epistle to the
Ephesians (vi. 17) as "the headband of salvation "
(περικεφαλαία τοῦ σωτηρίου ; in the A.V. called helmet).
It was distinguished from the white garment as
late as the ninth century, but now only survives in
the christening veil and amice. Raban Maur, A.D.
829, writes[28] respecting these two garments : "After
baptism he is clothed in a *white garment*, indicating

[26] De Eccl. Offic. i. 29.
[27] Reichel's Manuals of Canon Law, 47, 48, 213.
[28] De Cler. Inst. i. 29 ; ap. Gratian iii. Dist. iv. c. 91.

Christian innocence and purity. . . . . After the holy unction his head is covered with a *mystic veil*, that he may understand that he possesses the diadem of royalty and the priestly dignity." Pseudo-Alcuin, *i.e.*, Albinus-Flaccus (Epist. 90), says : " Then [*i.e.*, after baptism] he is clothed in a *white garment*, because of the joy of regeneration and purity of life and the glory of angelic splendour. Afterwards his head is anointed with the holy chrism and covered with a *mystic covering*, that he may understand that he now bears the dignity of kingship and priest-hood." So, too, the Saxon Pontifical quoted by Soames (p. 109) directs the bishop, in administer-ing solemn baptism, to give to each of the baptised (1) a white garment, and then (2) a chrism-band."

3. Although the white garment and royal head-band appear to have been the liturgical garments of all Christians, yet a difference in form and shape between those used by the clergy and those used by laymen seems to have manifested itself almost from the beginning. The earliest direct authority which I have been able to discover for the white garment being ordered for use by presbyters as a liturgical vestment is in the so-called canons of

" Det singulis stolam candidam et chrismale.

Hippolytus, which modern critics pronounce to be the canons of an early Roman Synod held under bishop Victor (190 to 199 A.D.). One of these canons, the thirty-seventh, prescribes : "When the bishop holds a liturgical gathering, let the presbyters who stand by him be clothed in white." Some two centuries later the Apostolical Constitutions (viii. 13) direct the bishop, before he makes the offering, to put on his shining garment (λαμπρὸν ἐσθῆτα). St. Jerome ("Adv. Pelag." lib. i.) considers it most conducive to God's honour for the bishop, presbyters and deacons, and all the ecclesiastical estate, to be clothed in white at the offering of the gifts. Gregory of Tours ("De Gloria Martyr." c. 20) speaks of "presbyters and deacons being present in great numbers, clothed in white." The Statutes of the ancient Church, which represent the practice of Southern Gaul at the beginning of the sixth century, direct the deacon to wear an alb only at the time of the oblation or of the Gospel reading.[30] Fortunatus, writing in the middle of the sixth century, speaks of bishop Germanus of Paris and all his clergy as apparelled in white,[31] and Isidore says

---

[30] Can. 41, ap. Gratian 1 Distinct. xciii. c. 19.
[31] Lib. ii. c. 10: Sed et hi bene vestibus albent.

that the dalmatic or sacerdotal robe was white and decorated with bands of purple.[31] Hugh de St. Victor in the twelfth century says[32] that deacons clothed in white raiment assist at the altar, that by the whiteness of their garments the purity of their lives may be signified.

The layman's white garment may possibly at first have been a garment reaching to the feet, but it very soon ceased to be such. Nay, more, it gradually grew shorter and shorter until it became a mere shoulder cape which was attached as a flap or curtain to the linen bonnet which represented the headband. Possibly the combination of the shoulder cape and headband in one may be of Gallican origin, but it was widely diffused, and is found alike in the chrisom of the baptised, in the layman's tippet, and the monk's cowl. That the chrisom, which was already in use in this country at public baptisms in the ninth century, was a combination-garment, may be seen

[31] Orig. lib. xix. c. 22: Tunica sacerdotalis candida cum clavis ex purpura. Liber Pontificalis in Acta St. Eutychiani says: He also appointed that whoever of the faithful should bury a deceased martyr should on no account bury him without a dalmatic or colobion of purple hue. At a royal coronation, ap. Maskell, Mon. Rit. ii. 25: "Then [the king] is vested in the sleeveless bodycloth (sindonis colobio) shaped after the fashion of a dalmatic.

[32] Maskell, Mon. Rit. ii. 244.

from the words of the Leofric Missal, which (p. 238) directs the chrisom to be placed on the top of the head (*posito chrismali in capite*), showing (as the name implies) that it was intended to serve as the chrism-guard or headband, but directs it to be placed there with the words, " Receive the white garment," showing that it also purported to be the white garment.    Similarly, the Evesham Book (Henry Bradshaw Society, p. 98) directs the abbot to place the chrisom on the infant's head (*super caput ejus*), but to do so using the same words, "Receive the white garment."

On the other hand, the white garment of bishops and presbyters was kept distinct from the headband or amice, and retained its length as a garment reaching to the feet.    In the vision which St. John describes as having beheld on the Lord's-day, when he was cut off from the accustomed service with his people, he writes of "seeing seven golden lamps, and in the midst of them One like unto the Son of man clothed in a garment reaching to the feet (ποδήρης), and girt about the paps with a golden girdle."    Commenting on these words, St. Irenæus,[34] A.D. 180, says : " He sets forth here something of the glory

[34] Haer. iv. 20, 11.

which He has received from His Father in what He says concerning the head; something in reference also to the priestly office, as in naming the long garment reaching to the feet." This comment proves that in the time of St. Irenæus, as also at the time when the Book of Revelation was written, the long garment reaching to the feet was regarded as distinctive of the priestly office. Eusebius,[35] moreover, in his sermon at the dedication of the great church of Tyre in 335 A.D., addresses presbyters as "Ye that are clad in the robe reaching to the feet." It seems, therefore, legitimate to conclude that in the fourth century only bishops and presbyters wore the white garment long.

Nevertheless, the clerical long robe, or white *tunica talaris*, the λαμπρὸς ἐσθής of the Apostolical Constitutions, must not be confounded with the coloured *tunica talaris*, or cassock, which was the clerical form of the Roman citizen's tunic. The former is now represented by the alb, the liturgical garment, the latter by the cassock or garment for ordinary wear.[36] The alb is common to all parts of

---

[35] Hist. x. 4.

[36] Leofric Missal, p. 258, directs the inferior clergy to wear casulae (*i.e.*, cassocks) and solemn vestments. *Id.*, p. 261, speaks of collets apparelled in black cassocks (casulae).

the Church ; the cassock is distinctive of the Roman clergy ; but whereas the Roman alb was a tight-fitting garment with tight-fitting sleeves, the Gallican alb or surplice was a full and loosely flowing robe.[37]

With the headband there was less room for variation in shape, save that the clerical headband remained a distinct vestment and has come down to us as the *superhumerale, amice,*[38] or graduate's hood ; whereas the layman's headband, having absorbed the white garment, has disappeared altogether, the only surviving relic of it being the curtained bonnet worn by working women in the field.

St. Isidore[39] in the seventh century mentions as general liturgical vestments, these two—the long

[37] Germanus ap. Duchêsne, 367, and Le Brun, vol. ii.

[38] The coronation ritual in Maskell, Mon. Rit. ii. 25, directs the king to be vested in a long sleeveless body-cloth, and his head to be covered with an amice because of the unction. *Id.*, p. 26, observes that originally the amice was a covering for the head.

[39] Etymolog. xix. 21 ; Alcuin de Divin. Offic. ap. Maskell, Mon. Rit. ii. 259: Poderis is commonly called alb. In the life of Thomas à Becket (quoted *ib.* ii. cli.) it is stated that he was buried in the hair-cloth which he was wearing at the time he was murdered. "And above these in the same vestment in which he was ordained, the *alb*, which is called by the Greeks *poderis*, and a simple chrism-cloth superhumeral (chrismatica), a mitre, stole, and handkerchief ; above which he had on archbishop-like a tunic, dalmatic, chasuble, pallium with needles [to fix it], a chalice, gloves, ring, sandals, pastoral staff.

white robe, which he calls *poderis*, and the amice or hood, which he calls *superhumerale*. The same two are mentioned in the ninth century by Raban Maur[40] as a group by themselves. At an earlier date even than Isidore, the Council of Braga,[41] A.D. 561, in decreeing that " all clerks shall minister with close-cut hair, having their ears exposed, and shall, like Aaron, wear a garment reaching to the feet, that they may be in glorious array," appears to have contemplated the use of no other garments than the amice and alb for general liturgical use, and to have directed the clergy to let down the amice behind, so as to expose the ears before commencing their ministrations, and to wear throughout them the long and not the layman's short alb. So also the Roman Order of the ninth century[42] only mentions two garments as worn by deacons and sub-deacons during the solemn service, viz., the alb and the *anagolagium*. The anagolagium,[43] which it orders to be worn only on solemn days, appears to be another name for the amice

[40] De Cler. Inst. i. 15.

[41] Ap. Gratian, 1 Dist. xxiii. c. 32.

[42] In Reichel's Solemn Mass at Rome in the ninth century, p. 37.

[43] Anagolagium appears to be a corruption for anabolagion = αναβόλαιον, an enveloper—*i.e.*, the enveloping hood or amictus. Similarly, in the Exeter Domesday, Devon Association's edition, p. 1140, excangiis and excanbiis are written on the same page for excambiis.

proper or clerical hood, the superhumerale of the Gallican Church.  For at Rome itself, amice (amictus) meant
something different, viz., the napkin  or *sudarium*
(called also *orarium* before  the  tenth  century,[44] and
possible subumblem[45] in the Anglo-Saxon laws), which
was put on under the alb to prevent its being soiled,
and to protect the chest and voice.[46]  As late as the
year 1402 A.D. we find in the inventory of St. Paul's
Cathedral [47] albs and amices enumerated for the use

[44] Duchêsne Origines du culte Chrétien, 376.

[45] Edgar's law, 33, A.D. 960 : "That every priest have a subumblem
under his alb when he celebrates mass, and every vestment decently
put on."  Bearing in mind the deep reverence of the Saxons for everything Roman, it seems more satisfactory to explain this law as ordering
the use of the Roman amictus or sudarium, rather than the Gallican
amictus or superhumerale, which was probably already in use.  The
Leofric Missal, A.D. 1024, directs the superhumerale to be first put on,
then the alb, and afterwards the girdle and stole.  On the other hand,
archbishop Gray's Constitution, A.D. 1250, mentions the alb first, then
the amice, and afterwards the girdle and stole.  According to Le Brun,
p. 43, the Roman practice about the year 900 A.D. was for the priest
first to put the amice or hood on over his head, tying it round the neck,
then to put on the alb and other vestments, and to proceed to the altar.
On reaching the altar he threw back the amice, and it fell hoodwise
over the shoulders.

[46] Le Brun, "Explication de la Messe," ed. 1777, p. 42, states that
at Rome the amictus was the neck-covering, the neck being usually
bare.  Its object, according to Amalarius, ii. 17, was to preserve the
voice for the praise of God.  He states that in some churches it must
have been regarded as the sack of penitence, to judge by the prayers
used in putting it on and taking it off.

[47] Sparrow's " St. Paul's," p. 39.

of the choristers as well as for the higher clergy; and the king at his coronation was vested in a long sleeveless rochet and amice, the latter, as the rubric says, being worn because of the unction.

### III.—BADGES OF DISTINCTION WORN BY THE CLERGY.

Besides the ordinary walking costume and the liturgical garments of the clergy, both of which seem to have been at first common to them and all Christians, we meet with others after the middle of the fourth century which may be best described as badges of distinction or official position. Such was the girdle worn in the East by clergy of all grades, in the Western Church only by the ministerial clergy. Such was the stole or scarf, worn at Rome only by the Pope, in the East by bishops, presbyters and deacons; and such was also the ceremonial handkerchief or maniple.

1. The girdle is properly an article of lay dress. It was worn at Rome by the officials of magistrates, but not by magistrates themselves, and hence when used by the clergy it was at first confined to deacons and the ministerial clergy, and was not worn

by bishops and presbyters. The Apostolic Constitutions (ii. 57) direct deacons to wear a girdle with
the alb when conducting the public service of the
Church. In the Gallican Church, nevertheless, the
girdle appears to have been regarded as a priestly
vestment, probably because the great High Priest in
the Book of Revelation is described as wearing a
girdle about the paps, and it was therefore worn
by the higher as well as by the lower clergy. On
this point a difference between Rome and Gaul
existed in the fifth century, as may be seen from
the letter of Coelestine[48] to the Gallican bishops
already referred to. Notwithstanding papal cen-
sure, the use of the girdle among the higher clergy
extended in the West, and was ultimately adopted
everywhere, probably as a consequence of the disuse of solemn services. For when the necessities
of the parochial system obliged presbyters to dis-
charge the deacon's functions as well as their own, it
became necessary for them to receive the deacon's
ordination as well as their own, and to wear the
deacon's vestments as well as their own.[49]

---

[48] Ep. 4, ap. Constantium p. 1067 ; Jaffé, p. 369. See note 10.
[49] Raban Maur. " De Inst. Cler." i. 17, says : " Lest the tunic should
hang loosely and hinder motion."

2. Another badge of distinction is the stole or scarf, but, as M. Duchêsne (p. 376) has already pointed out, this decoration appears to have been unknown at Rome except in the form of the papal

FIG. 3.

Roman consul. The broad scarf which goes round him is the *lorus*, and is probably the origin of the pallium. In his hand he holds the *mappula circensis*, folded up, ready to let fall.

pallium for the first ten centuries. It is true that before the tenth century the Roman clergy wore a vestment called orarium, but this orarium was not the stole. It was a garment worn *under*, not *over*, the sacerdotal vestments, and was only another name for the napkin or *sudarium*, the purpose of which was to prevent the alb from being soiled. On the other hand, the stole (orarium) in the sense of a visible scarf, was used as a badge of distinction in the Eastern Church not only by bishops but also by presbyters and deacons in the fourth century. The Council of Laodicea in 363 A.D. (Can. 22 and 34) forbids sub-deacons and readers to usurp the use of it. There seems, indeed, little reason to doubt that the bishop's pallium, or ὠμοφόριον, the presbyter's stole, or ἐπιτραχήλιον, and the deacon's stole, or ὠράριον were originally various modes of wearing one and the same decoration, which was probably introduced into the Church in the fourth century in accordance with the civil law requiring all officials to wear some distinctive mark of their office. Church officials in the East promptly complied with this law. The more conservative Roman Church did not adopt it, or at least only the bishop did, by wearing the pallium when it was directly given him by the emperor.[50]

---

[50] Duchêsne, p. 371, observes that "the fabricator of the so-called Donation of Constantine, late in the eighth century, regarded the pallium as an imperial concession; for he states that Constantine bestowed on Pope Silvester "the shoulder cloth (superhumerale), to wit, the band which usually encircles the imperial neck." The pallium was a long band of white wool draped round the shoulders [whence it was

Bishops passed the scarf round the neck and tied it, leaving one end hanging down in front and one behind. By presbyters it was passed half round the neck and crossed upon the breast. By deacons it was simply passed over one shoulder. Isidore of Pelusium,[51] A.D. 410, says that the episcopal stole, which he calls pallium, was made of wool, whereas the deacon's stole was made of linen.

called superhumeral by the Romans, a very different article from the Gallican superhumeral, hood or tippet], and hanging down before and behind. It was worn by the Bishop of Rome, and also by the Bishop of Ostia in the fifth century. The Bishop of Ravenna also wore it in the sixth. Pope Symmachus (A.D. 498–512) granted the use of it to Caesarius of Arles, and this concession was renewed by his successors. Gregory (A.D. 590–604) bestowed it upon the bishops of Syracuse, Messina, Milan, Salona, Nicopolis, Corinth, Justiniana Prima, Autun, Seville, and Canterbury. But it appears to have been thought necessary to obtain the emperor's permission before bestowing it on those who were not subjects of the Greek empire, which supports the view that it was originally looked upon as an imperial concession. Thus Vigilius (A.D. 538–555) applied for the emperor's permission before bestowing it upon Auxanius and Aurelian, bishops of Arles. Gregory applied for the like permission before bestowing it on the Bishop of Autun, but he does not appear to have demanded permission before bestowing it on the bishops of Seville and Canterbury, possibly, as Duchêsne observes, because Augustine of Canterbury was a Roman monk and a subject of the Emperor Maurice, and because Leander of Seville had been long resident and was well known at the Court of Constantinople. In the seventh century the Emperor Constantine II. himself bestowed it upon the Archbishop of Ravenna. Should it turn out that after all the pallium is the remains of the Roman toga, a reason for the imperial intervention in bestowing it upon outsiders will have been found.

[51] Ep. i. 136.

The biographers of Popes Agatho and Stephen III.
in the "Liber Pontificalis" [45] call the Pope's pallium his
stole.  St. Chrysostom, in his sermon on the prodigal
son, speaks of the linen stole (ὀθόνη) being worn by
deacons over the left shoulder when they conducted
the service (λειτουργοῦντες), and compares its waving

FIG. 4.

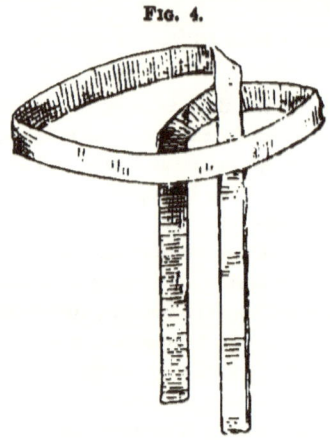

The *pallium*, as worn by a bishop.

motion as they move to and fro in church with the
waving motion of angels' wings—deacons being elsewhere called angels. [46]  The stole was also in use
in the Gallican Church.

The Council of Braga, A.D. 561 (Can. 2|3), directs

[45] Duchêsne, Lib. Pont. I. 354, 472.
[46] See Reichel's Solemn Mass at Rome in the ninth century, p. 20.

deacons not to wear their stoles (oraria) under their tunics (or albs) so that they are mistaken for sub deacons, but to wear them above the tunic over the shoulder. The Fourth Council of Toledo,[54] A.D. 633, mentions the stole (orarium) as a distinctive badge of bishops, presbyters and deacons. The deacon it directs (Can. 39) to wear his stole on the left shoulder, and (Can. 40) forbids him to wear more than one stole, and that "neither coloured nor embroidered with gold." The Third Council of Braga, A.D. 675 (Can. 3) forbids priests (sacerdotes, *i.e.*, bishops or presbyters) to celebrate mass without having on "a stole passed round the neck and crossed upon the breast." Similarly, Germanus of Paris[55] (A.D. 555–576) mentions the bishop's scarf or stole, which he calls *pallium*, and the deacon's stole, which he calls *stola*, agreeing in this use of terms with Isidore of Pelusium. And that he uses *pallium* and *stola* to express a form of scarf, and not, as we might have thought from the derivation of the words, to express a large vestment or gown, is proved from his own definitions. The bishop's *pallium*, he says,

[54] Can. 27, ap. Gratian Caus. xi. Qu. iii. c. 65.
[55] Quoted by Duchêsne, Origines, p. 378; Le Brun, vol. ii. p. 242 See Appendix.

is a band passed round the neck, with one end falling over the breast, terminating in a fringe. The deacon's *stola*, he says, is worn over the alb.

After the 10th century the use of the stole by presbyters as well as by deacons became general in the West, and spread up to the very gates of Rome. Nevertheless, within the city the ancient Roman practice for the priest to wear no stole long held its own, and when the Eastern custom was adopted it was adopted with a compromise. The stole was put on above the alb, but the dalmatic or planet was put on above it,[56] and to render this possible without inconvenience the ends of the stole were caught up, and after being drawn across the breast were confined by the girdle. When once the stole had become a liturgical vestment it received the same treatment as the pallium and at Rome was laid on the tomb of St. Peter the night before ordination.[57] In this country, as appears from Egbert's Pontifical, it was customary to bless the stoles for deacons and the

[56] According to "Liturgia Armena tradotta Venezia," 1854, the Armenian clergy put on first a tunic or dalmatic, and above this the stole. Above these the celebrant only puts on a superhumerale or large collar, resting on the shoulders, called *vagas*, and then a long flowing pluvial, which envelops the whole person and is not closed in front like that of the Greeks.

[57] Duchêsne, 376 note.

planets for presbyters at the beginning of the ordination service.[58] Various mystical meanings were then
assigned to it.[59] Still in its origin it appears to have
been a diaconal rather than a priestly vestment, a
worldly rather than an ecclesiastical decoration,[60] and
possibly on this ground the austere "Friar John," as
archbishop Peckham was wont to describe himself,
may have refrained from prescribing it as a Eucharistic vestment for the beneficed clergy of the Southern
province. Its use was no doubt enjoined when
carrying the Eucharist to the sick, but this by
the ancient custom of the Church was the deacon's
duty.[61]

3. The "Liber Pontificalis" mentions at the beginning of the 6th century a *pallium linostimum* or linen
scarf, as being worn by deacons at Rome and in the

[58] Maskell, "Mon. Rit." ii. 208.

[59] Alcuin, *ibid.* ii. 220. Orarium—*i.e.*, stole, so called because it is
given to orators—*i.e.*, to those who teach. "Let him who wears it be
reminded that he is under the yoke of Christ, which is light and
pleasant."

[60] Concil. Aurel. i. A.D. 511, Can. 20 : "No monk in a monastery may
wear a stole."

[61] Reichel's Solemn Mass, &c., p. 19. Synod. Dunelm, A.D. 1220, in
Wilkins, i. 559, directs the priest, whenever he takes the Eucharist to
the sick, to wear a "horarium seu stolam." Peckham's Const., A.D. 1279,
enjoins the same. It appears also from the ancient Ordo ad degre-
dandum sacerdotes in Maskell's Mon. Rit. ii. 332, that the stola was
deemed to be the badge of the deacon. See note 3.

suburbicarian province attached to the left arm.[61] This scarf Duchêsne thinks was an adaptation to ecclesiastical purposes of the *mappula circensis*, or ceremonial handkerchief, which was used by the consul to give the signal for the circus games to commence (Fig. 3). Its use was at first confined to Rome, so much so, that in the time of Gregory the Great (590–603) the Roman clergy protested against its being used elsewhere.[63] According to some ancient paintings preserved at Syracuse,[64] it was unfolded and held in the hand in receiving or presenting anything of value, and thus it came to be used not only by deacons and sub-deacons, but also by laymen[65] when-ever they made or presented offerings upon the altar. Hence, when the sub-deacon offered in place of the laity generally it became a distinctive badge of the sub-deacon.[66] In Germany it was called *fanon*. Amalarius (lib. ii. c. 24) and Ivo of Chartres ("Sermo

---

[61] Duchêsne, Origines, p. 369 ; Lib. Pont. pp. 171, 189, note 62 ; p. 225, note 2.

[63] Gregor. Ep. ii. 54, to John of Ravenna, ap. Gratian i. Dist. xciii. c. 22.

[64] Copied by De Rossi, Bull, 1877. Pl. xi., Duchêsne, 369.

[65] "Ordo Romanus in Muratori," p. 997 : " Whilst the singers sing, the people make their offerings, *i.e.*, bread and wine, and they offer on white napkins (*fanones*), first men, then women.

[66] Le Brun, p. 46.

de Signif. Indument. Sacr.") call it *sudarium*, and speak of its being used for the ordinary purposes of a handkerchief.[67] The Leofric Missal (p. 59) in the 10th century mentions it as one of the vestments of every officiating priest. The higher clergy in the Eastern and Gallican Churches wore in its place sleeves (*manualia, manicae*, Germ. Ep. 2, ἐπιμανίκια) of some rich material, and possibly the bracelets (*armillae*), in which the king is vested at his coronation, are a form of these.[68]

## IV.—ORIGIN OF THE LITURGICAL COSTUME OF THE THIRTEENTH CENTURY.

1. We are now in a position to account for the liturgical vestments prescribed for use in this country in the 13th century. They appear to be derived from three distinct sources. Some of them represent the ordinary garments of the Roman citizen, which, having in their origin nothing to do with religion,

---

[67] Robertus Paululus, De Offic. Eccl. i. 51 : Last of all the priest (sacerdos) puts the napkin (fanorem) on his left arm, which they also call maniple, and handkerchief (sudarium), by which formerly the nose and perspiration were wiped off.

[68] Maskell, Mon. Rit., ii. 29, 30, regards them as the equivalent of the stole.

D

were first retained in use as liturgical vestments and then introduced elsewhere for the same purpose, possibly much in the same way that the South African kinglet now adopts an occidental dress-suit and tall hat as a royal costume. Such are the tunic, dalmatic and planet.

Others are liturgical garments common to all Christians, and used with more or less variation in all parts of the Church, such as the alb or surplice and the superhumeral, amice, tippet or hood.

Others, again, are badges of rank or office, introduced as such first within the limits of the empire and then adopted elsewhere, such as the stole, the girdle in the West, and the maniple.

All ranks of the clergy and clergy everywhere wear the alb and amice or their equivalents. Roman clergy wear also the tunic and planet, and the higher Roman clergy the dalmatic as well. The stole as a badge of worldly distinction was worn throughout the empire, but in the Roman Church at first only by the Pope, in the Eastern and Gallican churches by all bishops, presbyters and deacons. The girdle, as the badge of ministerial duties, was worn by the deacon and those below him; the stole by the deacon, and the maniple by the sub-deacon; but their use was extended to presbyters when the presbyters were charged with the deacon's and sub-deacon's duties of making and preparing, as well as of consecrating the offering,

We see, nevertheless, from the 9th century Ordo, that the planet in the Roman Church was ordinarily laid aside by deacons when they entered the presbytery,[69] so that the dalmatic was the uppermost liturgical vestment of the Roman deacon.   Similarly, it was laid aside by the sub-deacon when service began,[70] so that the tunic was the uppermost liturgical vestment of the Roman sub-deacon.   Only the bishop and the presbyters continued to wear the planet during the celebration of the holy mysteries; and thus the planet, which was the Roman citizen's upper garment, came to be regarded as the distinctive

[69] Solemn Mass, &c., p. 37, line 38.   Le Brun, p. 57, observes that in Lent and other penitential seasons, for which joyous vestments were not suited, deacons continued to wear their planets in church, but rolled up and passed over the shoulder and tied in with the stole, so as not to interfere with freedom of motion.   A similar practice appears to be prescribed for presbyters who undertook to act as deacons, according to Theodore's Penitential II. ii. 11, A.D. 673, in Haddan and Stubbs, iii. 192 : " If a presbyter sings the responses in the Mass, or any one else, let him not lay aside his cope, but place it round his shoulders whilst he reads the Gospel."   Hugo de St. Victor in Maskell, Mon Rit. ii. 243 : "Deacons wear the stole on the left shoulder, and on fast-days the chasuble folded up over the same shoulder."

[70] *Ibid*, line 43.

vestment of those who consecrated the offering. The general use of the tunic as the sub-deacon's upper garment was not introduced before the 12th century.[71]

2. It remains for us to trace how the planet assumed the two varieties of form in which we meet with it in the 13th century : (1) that of the processional planet, cope, or pluvial; and (2) that of the abbreviated circular planet or chasuble. Allusion has elsewhere been made to the great change which came about in the manner of celebrating the holy mysteries between the fourth and the twelfth centuries. At the earlier date the conduct of the whole service rested with the deacon, and the functions of the presbyters were purely intercessory. Hence we hear in the fifth century of *Sacramentaries*, or books of prayers, for the priest, and of *Ordines*, or books of directions and *Responsales*, or response-books, for the deacon. A Service-book, as we understand it, containing both would then have been an anachronism. Before the 13th century, however, the needs of the parochial system had entirely changed the ancient use. The parochial incumbent was the presbyter and deacon rolled into one, who not only offered the people's prayers to God, supported by his

[71] Maskell, Mon. Rit., ii. 193.

own intercessions, but himself conducted all the details of the ceremonial worship. The active ceremonial duties which were thus thrown upon presbyters called for and produced a change in their upper Eucharistic vestment, the planet, and thus at all times when there was an offering to be made the planet became abbreviated into the chasuble.

It would be reading modern ideas into ancient history to suppose that the cloak (φελόνη) which St. Paul mentions (2 Tim. iv. 13) as having left behind him at Troas was a distinct Eucharistic garment, the chasuble. It was no doubt his paenula or planet, which he may have worn when celebrating the Eucharist, but also wore on other occasions. We know, however, from the writings of St. Augustine and St. Cæsarius of Arles, in the fourth and fifth centuries, that all persons were then required to be present at the Eucharist in their "best clothes," and this rule applied *a fortiori* to presbyters. Hence at Rome and in the East, where the planet or φελόνιον was the ordinary upper garment, it continued to be the Eucharistic vestment, only for this purpose they used the best planet they had. In the Gallican Church, however, where the mantle was the ordinary upper garment, the planet, no doubt derived from Rome,[72] was regarded as the distinctive Eucharistic vestment, and was called the *casula* or *amphibalon.* These names are first met with in the treatise of Germanus of Paris (A.D. 555–576). In this country, too, where the clergy dressed after the Gallican rather than the Roman fashion, the planet must have been in the seventh century regarded as the distinctive Eucharistic vestment. Hence when Wihtraed's Law (Law 18, A.D. 696) requires a priest " to purge himself before the altar in his holy vestment," there can be little doubt that the planet is referred to.

The distinction between the ordinary upper garment of presbyters and the planet used by them for Eucharistic purposes, which local circumstances brought about in France and England, was in the 9th century made universal by the decree of Pope Leo IV. in 847 A.D.,[73] which forbad the same planet to be used for ordinary wear and for Eucharistic

[72] Duchêsne, Fastes Episcopaux de l'ancienne Gaule, has conclusively shown that Christianity was introduced into France from Rome about the middle of the third century, and from France spread to this country.

[73] Labbé, viii. 33.

purposes, and from that time forward the ordinary
and Eucharistic planets are found to diverge in shape.
The original planet was a large circular cloak which
reached to the feet and envelöped the whole person,
whence the Gallican clergy appropriately called it
*casula*, or little house.[74] But this garment, when
made of rich material, was an exceedingly heavy and
inconvenient garment to move about in. Hence it
underwent a twofold process of adaptation. For
walking purposes it was cut open in front, so
that it ceased to be a close-cope, and was worn
like a mantle or cape, whence it was called cappa,
*cope* or *pluvial*; and such may have been the
Gallican mantle which Pope Celestine condemned.
It thus became the processional or ordinary planet
for walking, sometimes called gown (stola),[75] and
known in English Constitutions as "the principal vestment."[76] On the other hand, for Eucharistic purposes, when the presbyter had to dis-
charge the deacon's ceremonial duties as well as
his own, the planet was reduced in length and cut

[74] Le Brun, p. 53.
[75] Concil. Tribur., A.D. 895, ap. Gratian, Caus. xvii., Qu. iv. c. 25, quoted above note 13.
[76] See the quotations in the text at the beginning.

away at the sides to give free play to the arms, but retaining its original character as an all-round garment or close-cope, it retained its original name of *casula*. This casula or Eucharistic planet may be what Elfric, Bishop of Winchester, in the 10th century, speaks of as the " mass-vestment." After prescribing [77] that the priest shall have his mass-vestment that he may reverently minister to God as is becoming, he adds : " And let not that vestment of his be sordid, at least not to the sight," or, as it has been rendered, " at least not a cloak," as though the intention were to forbid the use of the ordinary walking-planet or cope. One of Edgar's laws (Law 46, A.D. 960) also ordains " that no mass-priest [*i.e.*, parochial incumbent] or minster-priest [*i.e.*, member of a collegiate chapter] enter the church or his stall without his close-cope, at least that he do not minister at the altar without his vestment." This injunction seems to refer in both cases to the Roman vestments. By the close-cope, the cassock or the walking-planet of the Roman clergy seems to be intended, and by the vestment the chasuble. But if the distinction between the walking-planet and the Eucharistic

[77] Canon 22, A.D. 957.

planet cannot be carried so far back as the 10th century, there can be no doubt that the English Constitutions of the 13th century distinguish "the

Fig. 5.

Bishop circa 1142 A.D.   Vested in *alb, dalmatic, chasuble* or planet, and *pallium*.  The sleeves belong to the dalmatic. The tunic is seen above the feet, below the dalmatic.

principal mass-vestment" from "the chasuble," and the distinction is still more clearly shown by the existing inventories, one of which, that of St. Paul's, goes back to the early part of the 13th century.

3. It may possibly jar upon the sentiment of some to find that vestments which have been deemed

specially indicative of Christian worship are but
survivals of the mighty influence of an extinct
empire; but let it not be forgotten that the ancient
view of all the adjuncts of public worship was, that
they were not valuable in themselves, but that they
were sanctified by prayer for the purposes for which
they were used. Hence, as Le Brun has pointed
out, the Greeks still bless each vestment every time
it is used. The Latins formerly did the same.[78]
Although the rule since the 13th century is that all
vestments must be blessed by the bishop,[79] yet the
priest is still required to say a prayer as he puts on
each one. Viewed thus, the source from which the
vestments are derived is of little importance except
from an archæological point of view; for, according
to the advice of St. Gregory, given to Augustine,
first Archbishop of Canterbury,[80] " If you have found
anything either in the Roman or the Gallican or any
other Church which may be more acceptable to
Almighty God, do you carefully make choice of the
same, and sedulously teach the Church of the

---

[78] Le Brun, p. 40

[79] Honorius III. to bishop of London A.D. 1220 in Decret. Lib. I.
Tit. xvi. c. 2, Lynd. 83, Constitution, 13 Edmund A.D. 1236.

[80] Baeda, i. 27.

English, which as yet is new in the faith, whatever you can gather from the several Churches. For things are not to be loved for the sake of places, but places for the sake of good things."

# APPENDIX

(TRANSLATION of a portion of the treatise of St, Germanus of Autun, ordained deacon A.D. 533, presbyter A.D. 536, by Agrippinus, Bishop of Autun ; consecrated Bishop of Paris A.D. 555.)

In what manner the solemn order of the Church is observed (agitur).[81]

And with what regulations (instructionibus) the ecclesiastical canon is honoured (decoratur).

Germanus, Bishop of Paris, wrote concerning the Mass. The first therefore and chiefest of all gifts of grace, the Mass, will be sung in commemoration of the Lord's death—for the death of Christ has become the life of the world—that by being offered it may avail for the health of the quick and the repose of the dead.

*The Priest's Vestments.*

The little house (casula) which they call all-round garment

---

[81] *Agere* and *actio* are technical terms used of the consecration prayer. Perhaps the heading might be freely rendered "The solemn order for the consecration of the Eucharist."

(amphibalum), which the bishop (sacerdos) wears, is sleevele[..]
unrent, without an opening, such as the people would not dare
wear.

The scarf (pallium) goes round the neck, breast and shoulder[..]
Kings and priests (under the law) wore a bright scarf-like (palleu[..]
garment; sacerdotal vestments end (or are fastened togethe[..]
with fringes.

It is the custom for bishops (sacerdotes) to put on gauntlet[..]
(manualia), *i.e.*, sleeves (manicae) like the bracelets (insta[..]
armillarum), by which the arms of kings and priests were confined [..]
therefore they may be made of any precious wool without th[..]
hardness of metal.

The tunic is a smallish (parvulum) garment, used for no other
purpose than for reproducing the offering (ad frequentandum
sacrificium).[82]

### The Deacon's Vestments.

The deacons wear albs or white tunics, which may be of silk or
wool.

The alb is not confined with a girdle, but hangs loosely down,
concealing the Levite's person.

The deacon wears a stole (stola) over the alb, but not in Lent
by way of humiliation.

### The Colours.

The book of the Holy Gospel is bound in red.

---

[82] Augustin De Civ. Dei. x. 6 has the same expression, Quod (sacrificium)
frequentat ecclesia. See Reichel's Short Manuals of Canon Law. The
Eucharist, p. 87.

The book of the Holy Gospel, as representing (in specie) the Body of Christ, is bound in red, a sign betokening His blood.

At Easter the Eucharist is covered with a covering (pallium) with bells [attached]; the priest wears white vestments at Easter.

*Printed by* BALLANTYNE, HANSON & CO.
*London and Edinburgh.*

www.ingramcontent.com/pod-product-compliance
Lightning Source LLC
Chambersburg PA
CDIIW022154020726

47496CB00008B/2708